The Dunderheads Behind Bars

The Dun

derheads

BEHIND BARS

PAUL FLEISCHMAN

illustrated by DAVID ROBERTS

CANDLEWICK PRESS

First edition 2012

Library of Congress Cataloging-in-Publication Data

Fleischman, Paul.
The Dunderheads behind bars / Paul Fleischman ; illustrated by David Roberts. — 1st ed.
p. cm.
Sequel to: The Dunderheads.
Summary: The Dunderheads — a gang of misfits with unique and unusual talents —
come to the aid of one of their own when Spider is falsely arrested for stealing jewelry.
ISBN 978-0-7636-4543-4
[1. Individuality — Fiction. 2. Mystery and detective stories. 3. Humorous stories.]
I. Roberts, David, date, ill. II. Title.
PZ7.F59918Dv 2012
[E] — dc22   2010048210

12 13 14 15 16 17 SCP 10 9 8 7 6 5 4 3 2 1
Printed in Humen, Dongguan, China

This book was typeset in Esprit.
The illustrations were done in watercolor, pen, and ink.

Candlewick Press
99 Dover Street
Somerville, Massachusetts 02144

visit us at www.candlewick.com

For Julian and Sadie
P. F.

For my friends
D. R.

When school ended, I thought we were done with our teacher, Miss Breakbone, forever. I thought summer would be boring. I thought I'd never see the inside of a jail cell.

Wrong, wrong again, and very wrong. Maybe the other Dunderheads shouldn't call me Einstein.

It all began exactly on July 12th, on page A-8.

I went over to Hollywood's to tell her the news. She's a five-star movie nut. Summer gave her time to catch up on her filing.

"Ashley Throbb-Hart? Here? Omigod! I just left my nine hundredth comment on her blog! We're like practically, you know—"

"People who've never met?"

She tried to mute me. It didn't work.

We ran downtown with Spider to sign up as extras. Half the city seemed to be there.

"How far to the front of the line?" asked Hollywood.

Spider's a champion climber. He shot up the nearest tall object. "Another half mile."

Then the tall object turned.

"Mannerless monkey!" shrieked Miss Breakbone. "Get off me this instant! I could have you arrested!"

Her brother was the chief of police.
We moved back a few places in line.

PARK SCENE
THROBB-HART
TAKE 1

We finally made it to
the front and got hired
for the park scene.

The hurricane scene was a problem
for Miss Breakbone.

We found Ashley Throbb-Hart's trailer
but could never get near her.

A few days later, I noticed some more news in the paper.

CAT BURGLAR STRIKES AGAIN

Priceless Necklace Taken From Third-Floor Bedroom

Citizens Demand Police Find Culprit

4th Jewel Theft This Week

I went to Spider's to see if he'd heard about it. I wasn't the only visitor.

"Thanks for the tip," I heard Chief Breakbone say.
Our old teacher grinned.

"Where's the evidence?" I demanded.

"The kid's a climber," said Chief Breakbone.
"I don't need more proof. Or some kid telling me
how to do my job."

"Especially this meddling mush-brain," said
Miss Breakbone.

I called a meeting of the Dunderheads.

"Spider's crazy about ropes,
not jewelry."

"Breakbone just wants to get back at us."

"I thought she toured with the Women's Wrestling League in the summer."

"We have to find the real thief," I said.

We visited Spider the next day. He had a twenty-pound weight on one leg to keep him from climbing out of jail.

"Don't worry," I said. "We'll get you out. How's the food?"

"Awful," he said. "And I heard my cell mate's in for cannibalism. So could you hurry?"

I thought . . .

I measured . . .

but I couldn't find a plan that worked. Then I remembered Google-Eyes was on vacation. I hoped her parents wouldn't mind if we used their empty house.

In the morning, I dropped by Clips's place. "Got an express order for you."

"Five hundred ninety feet of three-strand? By Thursday?"

"It's that or Spider's somebody's dinner on Friday."

"I'll try," he said.

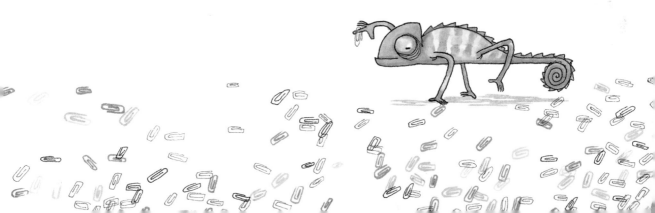

That afternoon, Pencil got to work on the flyer.

Wheels added autopedal to his bike that week. He made sure the word got out.

Junkyard combed his favorite alley.

Google-Eyes lives seven houses down from me.

Nails unlocked the back door with his right index finger.

We found her parents' bedroom upstairs.

Spitball got to work.

Junkyard had brought the jewelry box he'd found.

Clips attached the paper clips to it,

then we unrolled the strand all the way to my bedroom.

Everyone slept over.

We ran down the block.
Junkyard studied the ground
around the pine tree.

"We're too late."

"No problem," I said. "Switch to Plan B."
Then Chief Breakbone pulled up.

"We got a call on a burglary in progress," he said. "I had a feeling you half-pint hooligans were involved."

He didn't care that we were the ones who'd called. It took two cars to take us all to jail.

They confiscated Pencil's pencils,

clipped Nails's nails,

and put us all in together.

Luckily, Spider's cell mate was gone.

In the morning, we were taken to a judge.
"Surely you youngsters can't be mixed
up in this," he said.
"Actually," I replied, "we are.
But in a good way."

I explained about the flyers, the paper clips, and the
jewelry box we'd set out as bait.
"Fine work," said the judge. "Too bad he escaped."
"We knew that might happen," I said. "So I had
Spitball rub beef jerky on the room's floor. It'll be on
the soles of the thief's shoes. All we need to do is let
Spitball's dog track him."

The dog led the police from Google-Eyes's house all the way across town.

Finally, he stopped at one of the film crew's trailers. Which is how we caught the real thief —

the climbing . . .

crawling . . .

leaping stuntman

who'd been trying to win the love of Ashley
Throbb-Hart with stolen jewelry.

"What was the best part?" a reporter
asked us two days later.

"The judge telling Chief Breakbone
that he *could* use a kid's help."

"The mayor's Proclamation of Thanks."

"The private meeting with
Ashley Throbb-Hart."

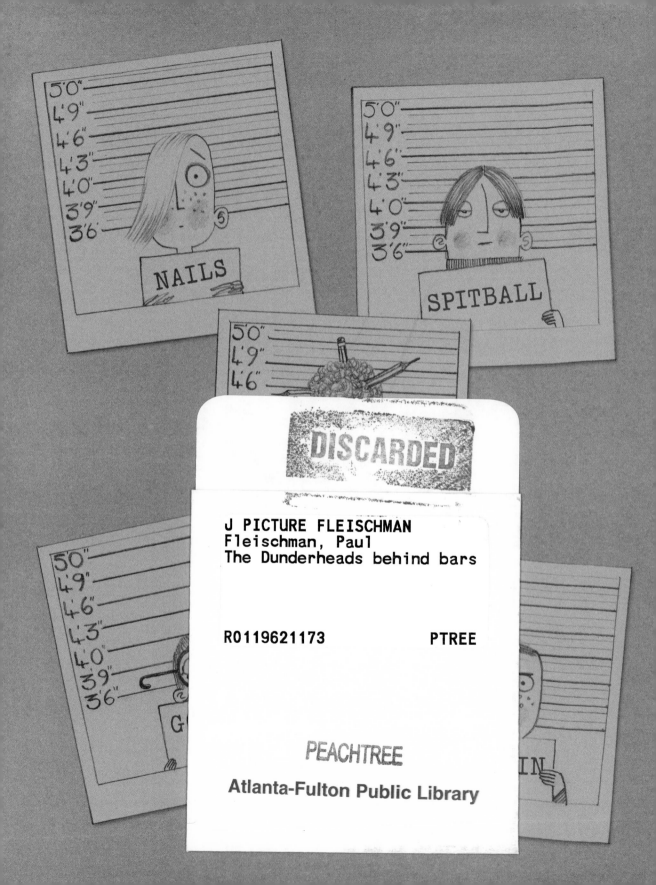